The Sylvan

The Sylvan

Story and Art by

Judy Vermillion Witt

For

Rosalie and John

May you find "magic"
in all *magic* and in everyone

Just—
IMAGINE

Judy Vermillion Witt

BRANDYLANE PUBLISHERS
White Stone, Virginia 22578

Other Books by Judy Vermillion Witt

The Center Ring with Pat Barner

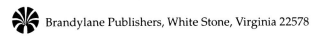 Brandylane Publishers, White Stone, Virginia 22578

The cover artwork is *Imagine* by Judy Vermillion Witt.

Library of Congress Cataloging-in-Publication Data

Witt, Judy Vermillion, 1941
      The Sylvan / Judy Vermillion Witt.
            p.   cm.
    ISBN 1-883911-07-9
      1. Aged men-Fiction. 2. Children-Fiction. I. Title.
PS3573. I9155S9 1996   95-39537
813'.54-dc20   CIP

To Jack, my true love.

Contents

Illustrations

Author's Notes

I kept asking myself why I wrote *The Sylvan* until I realized it was because I had to. I've wanted to write and illustrate my own book since high school when I made one for an art class. The muses have smiled on me, granted my wish and here it is!

The illustrations are paintings revealed to me by my imaginary friend, Sylvania. Whenever I wanted to create a new piece of art work, I talked with him about the next creation and soon discovered they contained a story. So I wrote from the images and discussions, weaving them with dreams and additional stories.

As a child I listened to fairy tales on a radio program called, "Let's Pretend." It began my lifelong love of making things up which sparked my imagination and later influenced my work as an artist. Believing imagery can have a powerful effect, I searched out ones that had a sense of mystery or inspired me. They lifted me and renewed my spirit. By following this path, my spiritual life unfolded within the pages of this book.

When I look through Sarah's eyes, I see the woods where I live as a place of enchantment filled with life and change. I am touched by its beauty, nourished by its presence. The seasons come and go as I move within the cycles. I know I can be myself when I smell the dark, dankness of the earth and listen to the wind whistling through the trees.

Sarah reminds me of dreams that make me whole and the world of the invisible while Sylvania leads me with his humor and wizardry ways. Together they have shown me how to share the fullness and aliveness of life in the writing of *The Sylvan*.

Judy Vermillion Witt

Appreciation

With a grateful heart, I give thanks to Barbara Goodman, Mary Sproles Martin and Rosalie West for helping me bring Sylvania and Sarah into the world through their "wizardress" skills in computer knowledge and editing expertise. And to my Mother, I'd like to thank her for the childhood memories of us roller skating together down the hill in front of our house, making snow ice cream and dolls of hollyhock blossoms. When I think of those happy times, it makes it easier to remember. . .Sarah.

Introduction

The Sylvan is a fable that revolves around a very imaginative child named Sarah who discovers and befriends a wise old man, Sylvania, living in a nearby forest. They teach one another about the essence of life as they take their magical journey together. So come with me and walk through the pages of a fairy tale time. A time that was, and is ongoing and without end.

Chapter 1

The Magical Journey Begins

Sarah stood before a heavy, wooden door that was partially hidden by trumpet vines, branches, and brambles. She turned around to see if anyone was watching and noticed slender white lilies growing in the middle of the forest stream. "That's strange," she thought, "I've never seen lilies growing there before." Pulling her attention back to the door, she lifted her hand to knock as the door swung slowly open. A garden courtyard of rainbow sights and sounds filled her view and an array of brightly colored birds flitted from flower to tree, their songs chorusing through the air.

A tiny house sat on the other side of the garden with a large oak tree that spread its branches over the rooftop, giving it coolness and shade. A tall turret stood within its vine-filled walls, and dark green boxes flowed with colorful blooms beneath the open windows. A porch ran along the front side so anyone sitting there could watch the fountain that occasionally sputtered and spewed as it attempted to flow into a sky blue basin. Little gold fish hopped in and out of the water in bright orange flashes. But the strangest sight of all was the stone bench made to look like a dragon. Its head lifted into the air as if it were taking in the view. Hung from its tail was a swing that squeaked back and forth in the breeze. Sarah's curiosity got the best of her.

She stepped inside the courtyard and slowly tiptoed along a wide stone pathway. As she moved forward, the festivities fell into a hush, then silence. Everything became very still. Sarah bit her lip nervously and rubbed her red sandal clean against her other white-socked ankle. She pulled her sleeve across her face and eyes, smearing the salty tears forming there. Prickly bumps of fear ran across her shoulders and arms as she gasped, "I'm scared. I think I'd better go."

As she turned to leave, the wind picked up and a breeze blew a soft whisper sound along the garden wall. "SA-RAH. . .SA-RAH. . ." She whirled around to see who called, but only a blue shadow darted across the courtyard entrance. Sarah's eyes were sweeping over the flowers looking for that someone who knew her name when it happened again. . . "SA-RAH. . ."

Suddenly, she had the feeling of being pushed from behind, a force that made her feet move towards the house and its darkened foyer. Once inside the shadows, her eyes grew accustomed to a cold hallway with steps that turned and spiraled, taking her around and upward to an unknown destination. She could not stop. She climbed the steps two at a time, her heart pounding in her ears. Breathless, she rounded the last turn and immediately stepped out of the dimness into sliced patches of sunlight.

Sarah stared in surprise at the specks of dust rising in the afternoon brightness. She was standing in a room with arched windows that opened to clouds and sky. A large wooden table laden with books and papers stood in front of the windows where she seated herself to gaze at the scene beyond. Farmlands rolled down to the full, deep river that flowed by the trees at the foot of the hill. Dogs barked in the distance while crows swung lazily about on the late afternoon breezes.

"Yikes!" Sarah suddenly remembered she was in someone's house—and it wasn't hers! What to do? She stood up and brushed her skirt smooth and thought, "Perhaps I'll be caught and punished for coming inside someone's house uninvited. I need to think about how to get out of here without being seen."

She turned from the window and found that a portion of the room was dimly lit, yet comfortable and inviting. Two chairs, unlike any she had ever seen, sat before an open hearth. As Sarah moved closer she realized what made them so different—they were trees! Branches curved and twisted into arm rests, roots spread into footstools and tiny wooden shoots formed an arbor to frame the top of the seats. As she took her place beneath the limbs, tiny lights twinkled and blinked above her head.

Sarah giggled to herself as she snuggled into the tree's familiar comfort and looked about the room. The fireplace was large and smelled of old fires, long forgotten. A tree stump table stood between the chairs and on its top sat a beautiful glass ball, pulsating with light, echoing the bright movement encircling the chair top. Sarah picked up the ball, placed it on her lap, and peered into it to find a smiling, elderly man looking directly at her!

Sarah was so alarmed she jumped, banging her head against the overhanging branches. "Who are you?" she yelled in surprise as she hurriedly returned the ball to the table.

The man replied calmly, "I am the Sylvan from the North Country, better known to my friends and neighbors as Sylvania. Welcome to my home."

"Your home?" Sarah gulped as she scrambled to stand. "This is your home?" She could feel herself acting dumber by the minute. She was caught, really caught now.

The voice rose from the ball. "It's all right for you to be here. I knew of your coming."

"You did?" asked Sarah. To herself she wondered, "How could that be?" She had told no one of her coming here or even of her leaving home.

The voice from the ball interrupted her thoughts. "Wind Messenger brought me word of your arrival. Your name was heard in the wind for many days. I listen to the weather this way too," he said. "In fact, my latest invention is about helping it to rain when the earth gets all crackly and dry and. . .oh, excuse me, we need to get acquainted. Please sit down, so we can have a talk."

Sarah returned to her chair as Sylvania asked her why she had come. She thought for a while and stuttered, "Uh. . .Uh. . .Well, I, uh, was taking a walk and, uh, I saw a door hidden under some vines in the hill.

I wanted to see what was on the other side, so I came in. I thought maybe I might find a new friend to play with now that it's summer and it's boring with nothing to do."

"Nothing to do? Nothing to do in the summer?" The glass ball began to spin and swing around the table in a golden, dizzy dance, stopping in the exact center of the table. Sylvania's face was pressed against the glass. His voice raised to new pitches of "Nothing to do?"

Feeling nervous, Sarah scrunched to the back of the tree chair.

"My dear, there is everything to do in the summer. Let's see. . ."

Sylvania disappeared for a few minutes and returned with a long list of items and events which he checked off as he called them out.

"Now then, there's star gazing and comet counting, cricket calls and grasshopper cries to listen to in the evenings as well as owls that hoot and howl in the night. Then there are sunsets to watch, fireflies to catch and put in a jar. How about a game of fetch with your dog, Scout?"

Sarah nodded, "Yes, those are fun things to do, but it's not like having a friend. You see, I'm lonely, really lonely. I moved to the country to live with my grandmother and I don't have anyone to play with. It's lonesome living in the woods without friends."

She could see the list fall from Sylvania's hands. He looked at her apologetically and agreed, "There is nothing like a friend." So, what's the problem? Let's be friends! We can go on adventures together to places both far and near, wide and here. Just thought I'd add a little rhyme to lighten the moment. Pretty good, don't you think, for on-the-spot verse?" He didn't give Sarah the chance to answer, but went on excitedly, "Oh, the fun of new discoveries, new lessons and new friends. We will be best friends, Sarah."

"How can we be friends when you live in a glass ball? You are so tiny and I am so big."

Sylvania seemed not to listen but suggested that she lean down and look into the glass at him. When Sarah bent over and looked at Sylvania, he asked her what she saw there.

"I see you."

"Anything else?"

"Well. . .there's a sign behind you that says, 'IMAGINE' in bright red letters."

"Huh?" Sylvania turned around to see if it was true and, sure enough, there it was: "IMAGINE," in red, glowing letters.

"What's IMAGINE?" Sarah asked.

Sylvania pressed his hand to his forehead as if trying to push out the answer. He thought for a few minutes and these few minutes grew longer while he paused to think some more. Finally, Sarah asked if he was taking so long because the sign was no longer there. Sylvania whirled around to see that the sign was gone.

Sarah laughed at the puzzled look on his face and watched him disappear into the ball to search for the sign. Returning to the chair, she suddenly felt sleepy. Her eyes were tired and heavy. Sighing a long sigh, she fell asleep from all the excitement.

* * *

Rain trickled on the window in big balloon droplets as she turned over in her bed. Lightning slashed through the trees like silver swords while thunder boomed across the hilltops. "IMAGINE. . .IMAGINE. . ." she whispered the words half aloud. "IMAGINE. . ." she thought she heard it in some far off voice that called to her through the rain. "Was it a dream?" she asked herself. Sarah sat up, swung her legs over the side of the bed and pushed her feet into her slippers. She rushed off to close the windows against the storm that thrashed against the house like wild stampeding horses!

"IMAGINE. . ."

Chapter 2

The Meeting

Sarah leapt from the back door and ran down the steps. She was on her way to the little house in the woods to see Sylvania. It felt good to run and stretch her legs as she bounded along beside the rushing stream. The faster she ran, the more aware she became of the mists that had begun to rise silently and steadily before her. Pausing to catch her breath, she stopped to watch the smoky vapors.

It was then she saw the doe standing at the edge of the woods looking directly and intently at her. Sarah stared in return at this wild, beautiful animal that had shown herself in the early morning light. They had caught one another by surprise. Not knowing what else to do, cautiously and simultaneously, they each turned to their own separate paths as if called by their own different lives.

Sarah's heart pounded in response to the surprise meeting. She wished she could have touched the warm brown fur, the tiny ears, and been a friend. But she soon stopped her musings and rushed on into the woods where the hidden doorway waited. Something wonderful and mysterious pulled her toward her destination.

Arriving at the front steps, she noticed a newly placed woodpecker door knocker which she quickly lifted and let fall with a loud BANG, causing the door to creak open. Sarah walked into the garden and called out in a small, unsteady voice, "Syl-van-ia." The bees answered in a low hummmmm. Slowly she gathered enough courage to scream, "SYLVANIA!!!"

With that, every squirrel on the roof ran for cover as the blue birds dove for their houses, each one fighting to get in first.

"Here I am again, and no one home."

Convincing herself that she was doing the right thing, Sarah remembered that Sylvania hadn't seemed to mind her being there before, so it must be all right this time, too. Creeping across the garden, she entered the dark foyer. Feeling her way along the unlit corridor and up the cold dark stairs, she found herself standing in the room with the view of the river.

It was as beautiful as she had remembered, but something was different. It was as if someone had been there just before her arrival--a presence just missed. Steam lingered above a bowl of soup sitting on the table and a teapot hissed from the stove. Some of the books stood in stacks piled to the ceiling while others lay strewn about with pages turned down to reveal wild scribblings and quotes in the margins.

Seeing the bowl, Sarah discovered she was hungry and sat down to slurp the fresh and delicious soup, forgetting to use the spoon. Having filled the empty space inside, she wondered again where Sylvania could be. Maybe he was in the garden or taking a walk in the woods. She sat still, thinking about what to do--when all at once, she heard it. Music. Fine, soft strands, then phrases rose and swelled in some faraway place, some distant valley, or was it some nearby room? Perhaps it was Sylvania rehearsing for a concert.

Leaving the table and empty bowl, she let the music guide her into a nearby hall where she discovered more doors. Puzzled, she stood before the first one and listened, but all was quiet. She turned the handle and found it locked. Above her head was a window, but she was not tall enough to see inside. The musical score still played on, but it was not coming from within. So, she moved down the hall to the next door.

Seeing her reflection in the door's coppery finish, Sarah became distracted from her search. Above the door was written, "I AM THE ROOM OF MIRRORS."

Sarah couldn't resist. She turned the knob and the door opened, revealing twinkling mirrors hanging from the ceiling, while others were partially hidden within the cracks along the walls. A mirrored floor gave Sarah the feeling she was losing her balance. She ran quickly for the open door and shut it behind her.

Once outside, she felt better. The soft, lyrical strains of music returned, calling to her from farther down the hall. She went on to the last door, where she paused, hoping to find Sylvania. It stood partially open, revealing a place Sarah wanted to be.

As she stepped into the room, she found crepe paper flowers blooming along the bottom of the walls. Little wooden men riding strange wild creatures swung before an open window and a colorful, paper lion mask hung above a tiny bed. A large orange and yellow trunk sat in a corner. Sarah opened and immediately closed it! The lifting of the lid set band music blaring with loud crashing cymbals and calliope music, causing the flowers to droop from the explosion of noises.

Sarah ran from that room with her hands over her ears, hoping Sylvania would come to the rescue, but he was nowhere to be found. Then she heard it again. . .the music that had started the search through the house. This time it was much louder and fuller. She felt compelled by the intensity of the song. She ran up a spiraling staircase at the end of the hall of doors, bringing the music closer. Once at the top, she expected to find Sylvania playing the chords and choruses, but she found herself in the turret room filled with more books and papers that fell in great white drifts. But the most amazing thing of all stood magnificently against one wall. An organ!

Sarah stared at the spectacle of keys, pipes, and stops. Keyboards rose in layers, and pipes of different shapes and sizes shot straight through the ceiling. Sarah wondered if they looked like smoke stacks on the roof. Finally, she knew where the music was coming from, but who was the mysterious player?

Feeling discouraged, she turned to leave when she saw a beautiful white owl sitting in the window. It winked at her and flew away. For a moment, Sarah thought its wings were gold, but reasoned with herself that it was only the sun catching the wings.

She returned to the steps and made her way back down the corridor, realizing that she was not going to see Sylvania, for it was time to leave. She felt very sad. A shiver passed over her, leaving her with an eerie feeling that someone was following her. She whirled around to catch that someone--but no one was there. She started to run, turned again, but no one stood behind her. Feeling more frightened, she ran full speed for the doorway. This time, a loud rumbling noise followed her and when she stopped, it stopped too. Then, she heard it-a tiny voice that said, "I'm down here."

Looking down, Sarah saw the glass ball sitting at her heel. She scooped it up and peeked into the gleaming glass to see a smiling Sylvania who said, "I've been following you. The next time you visit, look for me in the glass ball. I'll be sitting on the stump table between the root chairs. Just rub the glass and whisper, 'Lucky Star,' and we'll be together."

Sarah told Sylvania all about the mirrored room, the music-playing trunk, the crepe-paper flowers, and the wonderful organ she had discovered. She asked him if it was all real. To which Sylvania replied, "Everything is real in my house, Sarah."

* * *

The glass ball sat on the bedside table in the morning light. Sarah stared at its shiny roundness as she ran the soft cloth over it to remove the flecks of dust. "Was it really real?" she asked herself as she whispered, "Lucky Star, Lucky Star."

Chapter 3

Flying

Sarah loved to help Sylvania do the household chores. Today, she watered the geranium baskets on the front porch and noticed a bird's nest in one of them. She reached in to pull it out and throw it away. She and the sparrow had both been determined to have their own way. This time, the bird had won. There in the woven grass lay several tiny eggs. Suddenly, she remembered her grandmother's house and the ivy by her bedroom window. What fun it was to hear the squawking birds, watch them being fed with mouths wide open to receive a worm, see them being coaxed and pushed by their parents into learning how to fly. Now she could see it happen again. She had been given a gift—one she had almost thrown away.

Turning from the morning tasks, Sarah stopped for a moment to sit in the swing hanging from the tail of the stone dragon bench in the garden. She pumped her feet back and forth, making the swing go higher and higher. Her toes almost touched the sky! Her hair dragged the ground behind her and her dress blew in her face. She was sure she could fly above the treetops! She felt as if she were flying. Flying? She'd been thinking about it so much, she'd had a dream about flying. Well, it was almost like flying. She was suspended above her house in the dark night sky, lying down in mid-air! Her feet were pointing to a bright yellow moon as the bed sheets draped around her blew softly in the evening air. She wanted to talk to Sylvania about the dream, but when she arrived this morning, he was still asleep and had left a note for her under the glass ball. It said, "Hello. Up late. Worked on skunk perfume potion. Please water the plants. xxooxoo. S."

She was disappointed to find him napping when she had so many questions to ask. Maybe he was awake now and they could have some time to talk. She went in the house and checked the glass ball to see if he had risen, but he was still snoozing away. Sarah watched him for a few minutes. His arms were folded over his stomach as he rested peacefully in the curve of the ball. Sarah curled up in the root chair to wait for nap time to be over. She looked at the empty hearth and thought about the fires they would share as the cold winters descended upon the woods like a frozen giant.

Loud yawning noises quickly turned Sarah's thoughts to Sylvania's rising. He stretched out his sleepiness. Z letters appeared on his long white nightshirt and he kept slapping his watch to stop the buzzing alarm that pierced the air like bothersome mosquitoes. Sylvania began swinging his arms in flying motions, almost convincing himself that he was being attacked. He grabbed his wrist and stopped the terrible noise. "Silence!" he insisted. Sarah began to laugh. He could do the silliest things and not even know he was doing them.

"Sylvania, I need to ask you a question."

"O-o-no-not now, Sarah." He protested that he hadn't had his morning cup of coffee and he couldn't get started without it.

Sarah ran to the kitchen and found a jar that read, "INSTANT." And, sure enough, it was ready in an instant. She ran back to Sylvania with the cup of coffee which shrank in size when she placed it before the glass ball. Slipping through the glass, it flew to Sylvania who gulped down the black liquid, proclaiming that he felt much better, thanks to Sarah.

"Now, what was that pressing question you had for me?" he asked as he leaned back into the curve of the ball.

"Uh. . ." stammered Sarah, "Uh, it's not really a question, I just wanted

11

to tell you about the dream I had when I was sort of flying."

"Sort of?" inquired Sylvania.

"Yes, in a way, it was like flying." Sarah proceeded to tell him about lying in the air, suspended before the moon. She told him she felt full of the moon and stars, their beauty all around her, comforting her, reassuring her in gentle breezes, as if from some other world. Sarah paused in the remembrance of being part of something words could not describe, which had left her with a feeling of gladness in being alive. Sylvania sat in silence. He knew Sarah had discovered the true meaning of her dream.

Chapter 4

Keeping Watch

Sylvania and the owls called to one another making the H-O-O-O-A-A sound echo through the woods and into the starry night. Although it was a lonesome sound, Sarah didn't feel lonely because Sylvania was sitting in the glass ball beside her as they listened to the night noises. They could hear her dog Scout in the distance splashing in the creek looking for rocks, so they could play a game of fetch in the morning. Scout was a silly dog who ran after almost anything, especially rocks and sticks. He was always eager to play and have fun. That was what she liked about him the most, except when they sat together on the front steps looking intently across the meadow and into the woods, each speaking to one another without sounds or words. It was a strange thing that happened between them, some silent language of their own as if they knew one another in some inexplicable way. Then, both would return to being themselves and go about their day.

Sarah often felt that the unexplainable, unspoken language between her and Scout might be called love. She wasn't quite sure, so she asked Sylvania about it.

"Love comes in a myriad of forms, Sarah, but I think you have stumbled upon one of them. Remember that feeling, for it will come again and you will be reminded of what Scout gave to you so you can recognize it in yourself and others." Sarah smiled at the reassurance he gave her in discovering something special.

The evening carried that heavy feeling that only summer could heave upon the land, filling it with crickets fiddling and tree frogs bellowing. She thought it funny the way the squeaky sound of the crickets matched the squeak Sylvania's rocking chair made each time he leaned forward. It looked rather strange to watch him rock inside the glass ball. Sarah wished he would come out and sit with her on the porch, but she knew better than to ask. At that moment, lightning darted across the sky in the distance, as if to confirm her thoughts.

"Going to rain," Sylvania announced. "Can you smell it?"

Sarah breathed deeply and took in the sweetness that clung to the air. "Is that rain-smell?" she asked.

Sylvania nodded that it was. She asked him how he knew it was going to rain. Sylvania sat up straight and unbuttoned his shirt to reveal a weather vane imprinted on his chest. They both laughed, thinking it quite a joke.

The H-O-O-O-A-A sounds began again, reminding Sarah of her recent visits with an owl. Lately, as she returned home in the evenings after visiting Sylvania, the owl would be sitting in a tree or flying just ahead of her. Sarah had begun to look for the bird and waited for its arrival or listened for its call to give her direction. Walking along, she would glance up and there it would be! She was always surprised to find its presence nearby. Sarah felt as though she and the owl had been friends for as long as she could remember. Even though the bird made surprise visits, Sarah had the uncanny feeling it kept an eye on her during the day. It had become her companion.

As she listened to the hooting in the distance, she suddenly thought about being in Sylvania's upper turret room for the first time looking at the beautiful organ amidst the flurry of books and papers. It was there she had caught a glimpse of an owl sitting in an open window. At first it had appeared white, but as the sun slanted across its face, it glowed pale yellow in the afternoon light and winked at her before it spread its golden wings and flew away.

14

Immediately she knew! It was as if she had been struck by the bolt of lightning now dancing in the woods. "I've got it!" she exclaimed.

If he could sit in a glass ball, surely he could change himself into an owl. She turned to ask if it were true, but the glass ball was nowhere to be found. Only an old blue rocking chair rocked silently on the porch in the summer night.

THE GOLDEN THREAD

H-O-O-O-A-A. She heard the faraway cry.
The bird was singing her a lullaby.
Her eyes grew heavy, her breath fell deep.
She knew it was the owl who sang her to sleep.
He came to the window, then sat on the bed,
Lifting her lightly, kissing her head.
He carried her swiftly out to the sky,
Up through the clouds to the stars on high.
It filled her with joy, to sit on his wing,
To hear all the music, the heavens could sing.
She danced in the air, she flowed with the song,
To the great symphony sound that pulled her along.
Then, the great bird showed her one very last thing,
It was golden, a circle, one tiny gold string
That let itself spin inside and out,
Throughout the universe, it fell all about.
It encircled the people, this one golden thread,
Holding them together, invisible some said.
Remember it well when the owl cries call,
This one golden thread belongs to us all.
She flew on his back and returned to her bed,
Softly and silently, wrapped in the thread.
When she awoke on the morning's new day
There on her finger, a gold ring lay.
Inscribed in its circle this message was read,
Love is the string, the one golden thread.

16

Chapter 5

Wildflowers and Dragonflies

WHAM! WHACK! POW! Sarah had been trying to catch dragonflies for days. She hid in the wildflower garden and waited for one to land. Then she crept, ever so quietly, behind them and BAM—the net landed right where they had been! She wanted to capture one—just one! That couldn't be too much to ask. But it was. She gave up. She found a book about dragonflies and learned they had superb vision and extraordinary speed. But it wasn't their eyes or wings that caused Sarah to fail. Somewhere inside of herself, she knew something that beautiful should remain free. So she learned to sit quietly in the garden and watch them darting in and out among the flowers, the sun catching prisms on their wings. While following their escapades, she often heard the familiar strains of music coming from the turret room. When this happened, she would go there and find it empty. It left her with the feeling that someone was playing a joke on her, but she always went hoping to see who played the beautiful music.

Today was no different from all the others. The music lured her from the garden. She ran through the house, up the stairs, along the corridor of secret rooms, up the spiral steps, and to the closed door where the organ music rocked the walls and lifted the room. It filled Sarah in a way that made her feel as if every note was inside of her. She closed her eyes and listened with her whole self. She became the music, letting it touch something magical near her heart. She wanted to laugh and cry at the same time. Everything was happening at once.

Reaching out, she grabbed the doorknob, turned it, and yanked the door open, revealing the player and a room dazzling in sunlight. Sarah couldn't believe her eyes. His back was turned toward her and his hair swung in wild arcs as he reached for the flower petal stops and swayed to the enveloping music. The bird nesting in the opening of one of the pipes held on for dear life for fear of losing the nest and all of her children to come. Dragonflies swarmed around the sheet of music sitting above the keys. They flew along the lines, rested as the notes and became the song. Finally, with great gusto, the last note was struck. Ringing into silence, it moved along the rafters and rose like smoke through the chimney.

The recital was finished. The player wiped his brow and turned to face a very startled and mesmerized Sarah who stood with her mouth agape.

"Hello," she managed to whisper as Sylvania rose from the stool and shot straight into the air. He let out a yowl, causing Sarah to grimace and shut her eyes as tightly as she could. He yowled and yowled some more. Finally, she risked opening one eye to find Sylvania standing with his hands on his hips—smiling.

"I did not know of your arrival. You really gave me a fright!"

Sarah waited a few moments before making a reply. "I looked in the glass ball, but you weren't there, I said 'Lucky Star' one hundred times and you still didn't come, so I went to the garden to play. When I heard the music, I came in to find out who was playing. It was you! You can live outside of the glass ball! You are real!"

She stepped closer to him, and touched his shirtsleeve to feel his realness.

"Yes, I am real, real as rain and I'm never going back to the glass ball again!" he sang.

"You mean you won't be little anymore and I won't have to look for you in the glass ball ever?" she asked.

"That's right." he grinned.

Sarah was so excited she hopped around the room like a bug on a hot rock! Even the dragonflies got into the act. They hummed little tunes in their tiny voices and danced in chorus lines across the floor.

Everyone was happy with the news.

Chapter 6

The Secret

Every step caused a little flame to appear on the path, lighting her way through the settling darkness of the forest. They took her safely to Sylvania's front steps where he sat patiently waiting for her arrival.

Rushing toward him, she exclaimed, "Sylvania, did you see what I saw?" He acknowledged that he had with a large grin and an "Un huh."

"How did the lights come on?" she hurriedly asked.

"It's a secret," he answered through his continuing grin.

"A secret?" Sarah frowned.

"Yes. The secret is in you."

Sarah never quite knew what to say when Sylvania spoke in ways that were more like puzzles than answers. She sat down beside him and watched him puff on his pipe. The smoke hung lazily about their heads, reminding Sarah of burning leaves in the fall. She pondered the word "secret," wondering what it meant. Secrets had to do with surprises and gifts. It had to do with not telling someone something special you know.

Sylvania interrupted her thoughts by trying to explain that a secret can lead to discovery, often about one's self. He told her to run and hide behind a tree to see what happened to the candlelight. Sarah took off, running down the path as the little lights came on and glittered in the grasses. Jumping behind a tree, she looked into the woods and along the walkway to find everything dark. Returning to the path, she found the lights reappearing and by running back and forth, she created a dance of darkness and light. A rhythm came from within, helping her to move in joyful outbursts. She twirled, she stood on her tiptoes and leapt into the air. She spun in circles and swooped her arms all around as if they were great bird wings ready to spring her from the earth. Breathless, she fell to the ground in a heap of broken giggles as Sylvania applauded the performance.

Hopping up, Sarah ran to Sylvania and sat down beside him exclaiming, "I know what made the little candles light. I made them come on. . .didn't I?" she heard herself ask. "Wait a minute. How did I do that?"

She looked up to see if Sylvania had some answers, but he seemed to be waiting for her to find some of her own. This wasn't going to be easy. She stared at her shoes, rested her elbows on her knees and cupped her hands under her chin.

She looked as if she was thinking about it.

"O.K. try to come up with something. Let's see. . .uh. . .a secret about self. . .myself? Yes, myself! What kept the path lit? Now that's a good question. Funny thing is—I know why it went dark, but I don't know what made the lights come on. Everything was without light because I was hiding. Hiding? Something about hiding. . .

"Sylvania, is the secret about hiding?" she asked.

Sylvania nodded that it was.

"Hurrah! I have a hint," she thought.

Sarah shut her eyes and frowned. Finally, an answer came to her. She tried to remember what happened to her while she ran back and forth in the woods.

"When I hid behind a tree, I couldn't see anything, not even myself. I couldn't find myself anywhere. But when I was on the path and it was lit, I could be myself. It made me very happy!" Sarah said to herself.

She leaned next to Sylvania and said, "I think I know what it is I need to know. It's just about being me—being Sarah."

Sylvania turned to her and smiled his deepest smile of appreciation for her.

The Secret

"It's true, Sarah. It's easy to lose yourself. Just remember your own special uniqueness, just like the woodland animals. Each of them has something wonderful and different to offer and so do you. All creatures have a special spark that keeps their path lit."

As Sylvania spoke, Sarah looked at the small candles sitting by the steps. The little flames tilted as a breeze blew in and around them. The light had gathered itself about them, sending the shadows to play in the darkness beyond. She hoped she would remember this night forever—the night she danced the dance of lights.

22

Chapter 7

Moon Night

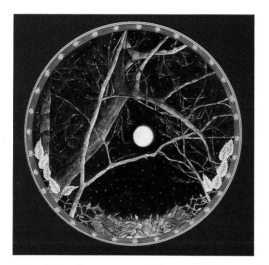

Sarah was making wishes—wishes to be with Sylvania. Tossing and turning, she began to cry. "I wonder what Sylvania does when he can't sleep. Does he read bedtime stories to himself or listen to music? or. . .does he wonder if I am asleep?"

The tears slid down her chin as she felt the moonlight peeking at her from beneath the window shade above her bed. She thought for a moment about the full moon that shone clear and cold in wintertime. She remembered the pale beech leaves that clung to the branches until springtime winds brushed them to the ground.

"But the full moon of summer looks different to me," she yawned. "I like the round, warm, creamy moon. It's like Sylvania's ball," she thought as she drifted into sleep.

* * *

. . .The glass ball glowed softly in Sylvania's hands as she peered into it, seeking her dreams. The figures were beautiful, ethereal. They were transparent—seen, yet not seen. Their feet never quite touched the ground, which gave them the appearance of floating from one place to the other.

* * *

The "invisibles" had been sent to guard the sharp curve in the road and prevent travelers from harm or warn them of great danger. Their presence was reassuring and comforting to those who had seen them gathered by the side of the road.

Not everyone saw these "beings," but many spoke of having traveled safely on the dangerous turn during terrible weather and harsh storms. Blinking lights and bright torches appeared during dense fog and heavy downpours. It was believed they could see around curves and beyond.

Waves and bows greeted those who passed them on the twisting road. Banners of good wishes were followed by signs of "Salutation." Their

favorite pastime was to celebrate and rejoice. During the Winter Festivals, they would sing lovely choruses of music and carry tiny lit trees to help travelers along their way. Sometimes their songs carried through the valley, across the rooftops, and into neighboring homes, which made everyone wonder what they were hearing and from where. Every year people would ask, "Have you heard the singing voices yet?" They would wait, anxious not to miss the melodies that flowed across the cold winter skies.

Often, fires could be seen blowing sparks into the evening as these figures danced around the flames, or in summer, one could hear them hopping and splashing into puddles lingering beside the road following rain. Their vigilance was never failing, for several watchful eyes were always left in attendance while the others entertained or joined in the festivities.

A large tree stood at the bend in the road and gave shelter to these guardians. Their children swung from its branches and climbed within its leaves and along its arms. It provided shade from the sweltering summer heat and glistened with icicles during freezing weather. In the fall, the tree spread its brilliant blanket on the ground, giving the little ones a playground piled with colors.

They loved the tree. It was their friend. They put their arms around it, drawing strength from its wide voluptuous trunk. For fun and enjoyment, the "invisibles" decorated the tree with small, paper-white messages, telling of fortunes and giving advice.

Often, at dusk, they could be seen floating across the treetops when it was time to replace those who were weary from watching and waiting. These "invisibles" kept everyone safe as the night closed the day. Darkness beheld their beauty. They took on the appearance of a pale blue and smoky-like quality that blended into the shadows and moonlight.

Some people doubted their presence, but those who knew of their protection discovered the road to be less difficult to travel. Others believed in them because they had seen and heard them as children in the "world of in-between" where sleep is just beyond and awake is just behind. In this place, the beautiful beings hummed lullabies and whispered, "Hush, hush" and, "Now, now" to comfort and cover them with visions, while putting them to sleep. Their tasks were never finished. They took danger and made it safe, offered peace where there was fear, and instilled trust in the life of the invisible.

Chapter 8

Wonderment

They sat in the swing suspended from the tail of the stone dragon bench and ate delicious, juicy tomato sandwiches. This was their favorite summertime meal. They gulped and slurped with loud sounds of "Ummm-umm-umm," each savoring the tangy sweetness of the home-grown tomatoes. In between bites, Sarah told Sylvania about her grand-mother who once lived in the mountains and called "tomaytoes, tomahtoes."

"ToMAYtoes?" snickered Sylvania. "ToMAHtoes?"

He laughed and Sarah laughed with him until they had swung them-selves to the ground in fits of laughter, repeating "toMAYtoes, toMAHtoes" over and over in a sing-song fashion. Just as they were about to calm down, one would catch the other's eyes and the laughter would burst out all over again. Finally, Sylvania hid his face in his hands and Sarah cradled her head in her arms as they lay on the ground to get hold of themselves.

Sarah managed to speak first.

"Sylvania, this is silly." He just smiled, wiped his eyes with his shirt sleeve, and stood up, brushing the grass and dust from his rumpled pants and shaggy hair.

"Laughter is good for the soul," he replied as he pulled a piece of grass from his mouth and moved to the swing. He pushed it back and forth, bringing on a screeching see-sawing sound. "Must get around to oiling this someday," he half muttered to himself.

Sarah sat up and pulled a piece of long flat grass, placed it tightly between her thumbs, and blew on it to make a loud whining whistle.

"What's soul?" she asked. The swing's screeching noise stopped. Sylvania played with his whiskers while he pondered the question.

Finally, with a scratch behind his ears and a hurrumph or two, he replied, "Well. . .I'm not really sure what it is. It's a mystery of sorts. . .I think it's like spirit or maybe it's like taking a drink of sweet water and the sweetness is the soul of the water."

Sarah sat very still watching the little bees hover above the clover blossoms and thought seriously about what Sylvania had just said. There seemed to be more about "soul" than she realized.

"Remember how we once talked about light?" Sylvania continued. "Well, soul is the light inside of us and it shines around us. Sometimes, you can see it glow in a certain way or you can see it come smiling from people's eyes. I would say it's what carries us. I believe that's some of what soul is, Sarah." He leaned back into the swing and the screeching see-sawing sound began again.

"I give up. I'm going in the house to get some oil to quiet this thing." Sylvania's leaving gave Sarah time to think over his answers. She heard him banging around the house and finally returning down the stairs. He stepped outside with a huge red can that said, "OIL" and squirted every screw and hinge in sight. He took his big handkerchief and wiped everything clean. Feeling as though he had accomplished a great feat, Sylvania brushed his hands together and proceeded to settle down for a quiet swing.

Just as he sat down and pushed off, the see-sawing sound began its musical screech all over again. Sylvania's eyes popped open in surprise and Sarah fell back into the grass, flinging her arms out as if to surrender to the laughter that overtook her.

She laughed so hard she got the hiccups. She tried to hold her breath

27

to make them stop, but it didn't help. In between laughs and hiccups, she opened her mouth to ask for a drink of water and out flew an opulent luminescent bubble filled with a beautiful purple-pink dragonfly that drifted into the air toward the flower garden. This time it was Sarah's turn to have her eyes pop in surprise! She started once again to ask for a drink, but as soon as she opened her mouth, a flying fish flew from her lips! In disbelief she watched it fly toward the fountain that stood nearby and take a dive into the bubbling pool.

Dumbstruck, Sarah could neither speak nor move! "Where did they come from? How can this happen?" she asked herself.

Sylvania slapped his knee. "They came right from your soul. Yes, indeedy, that was spectacular! Wonders never cease!" Leaving the swing, he knelt in front of Sarah and waved his hand in front of her face as if to see if she was still there. "Hello? Anyone home?" he called out as he gave her a friendly nudge. Sarah blinked a few times. Her face was pale and her mouth still hung open from this shocking event. Sylvania picked her up and placed her gently in the swing, letting her rest against its back. He went to the fountain, dipped a gourd into the cool waters and returned to her with the drink she had needed.

Handing her the gourd, he teased her, "Well, that's one way to get rid of the hiccups!"

Sarah took a few sips, still unable to say a word. Sylvania tried to comfort her by telling her about the strange and wonderful things that took place in his garden and how she was a part of the mystery that moved and lived there.

The color began to return to Sarah's cheeks. She heard Sylvania asking her if she would like to hear a story about a little fish who was given wings. Sarah gave a wistful little smile and nodded that yes, she would like to hear that story.

HOW THE LITTLE FISH GOT WINGS

Once upon a time and not so long ago in a land not so far from here, there lived a very unhappy little fish. He lived in a pond and swam to its edges to look up at the sky and all the tall grasses growing by the banks.

Every day he would long to leave the water and fly. Fly? The poor mother fish tried to tell the little fish that he didn't have wings, that he could not fly. It did not matter. He wanted to fly.

The little fish swam to the very top of the water and lept great leaps into the air, hoping that one day he would simply take off and never return. He could see himself swirling and circling above the pond, doing nose dives and even flying on his back. Oh, it would be a glorious thing to fly. Whenever he talked about it to his mother, she just shook her head and dabbed her eyes with her big blue handkerchief. But the little fish never lost hope.

One day he saw a beautiful dragonfly land on top of the water to taste some bugs. The dragonfly was so lovely, the fish could not take his eyes from her. Her wings were loveliest of all. All the little fish could do was stare at how fast they beat and wonder how fast they must fly.

Time passed. The little fish and the dragonfly became friends. The dragonfly shared all her adventures, where she had been, how far she had flown, and how wide and long her vision could be. All the little fish could do was wish to travel with the grand and beautiful dragonfly.

Finally, he could stand it no longer. He swam to the very depths of the pond to find the Frog King, who might be able to help him. He found the old frog gurgling in the muddy pond floor, his eyes bulging just above the mud. When he saw the little fish, he asked him, "Little fish, why are you here? Have you come to bother me and interrupt my rest?"

"No," replied the little fish. "I've come to ask for your help."

"Are you in trouble?" asked the Frog King.

"Oh, yes, sir, I am. For you see, I want to fly and I have no wings."

The Frog King laughed so hard he almost drowned from swallowing so much water. This near drowning made him quite angry and he began to shout and scream.

"Leave my domain!" he bellowed.

But the little fish did not give up. "Please, oh honorable one. You, who are most knowledgeable, can help me find my wings."

"Being king of the pond is not easy. The little fish is right," he thought, "I have much knowledge. Since I am king of the pond, I should be able to think of how this little fish can have wings." He thought and thought.

"Come back tomorrow and I'll have the answer," he gurgled.

The little fish swam away, delighted that the next day he would have wings to fly.

He told everyone the news, even his mother, who cried and cried because she knew the king was humiliated by the impossibility of the request. Now the whole family was to be put to shame. The little fish told his fish friends, but they made fun of him and laughed at him behind their fins. He could not wait to tell the lovely dragonfly. He swam to the water's surface where he found her waiting for him. The sun glistened on those wonderful wings he so adored. She flitted and flew to show off for him, while he watched from beneath the water.

"Come back," he shouted. "I have some wonderful news! The Frog King will tell me tomorrow how I can get wings. Then you and I can fly together forever."

The lovely and beautiful dragonfly smiled at him, for she, too, knew this would never happen. She only said, "I am glad we are friends."

The next day, the little fish swam as hard as he knew how to the bottom of the pond. He had been awake all night thinking about his wings. What size would they be? What color and shape? He knew that once he had wings he would be able to fly because he had imagined himself doing so for such a long time.

He found the Frog King sitting in his usual muddy hole wearing a bright golden crown. It shone above his bulbous eyes.

"Oh, great King, I have come at last to find my wings. What is the answer? When will they be mine? Can I see them now?"

The Frog King gurgled from his muddy seat, "In order for you to have wings, you must destroy the dragonfly and bring it to me for my evening meal. Then you will have wings."

With that, he slid down beneath the mud, leaving his crown floating on the muddy mire.

The little fish could not believe his ears. This was impossible! How could the king make such a request? The little fish thought briefly about the mission the king had given him, but he knew he could never do such

30

a terrible thing. His dream was over. Huge tears filled his eyes. The sadness of knowing he would never be able to leave the pond and see the world was more than he could bear.

His mother came to him when she saw his sadness and wrapped her big blue handkerchief around him to ease the pain. But nothing could help. He would never have wings.

Drifting away, he slowly slid through the water alone. His body felt like stone. For days he hid in the muddy waters and lay along the dark bank, knowing nothing mattered anymore. Little bubbles rose from the water where he lay and made their way to the top where the dragonfly anxiously awaited him. It had been a long time since she had seen him. She was very worried. She asked the minnows if they had seen him, but they only shook their heads as they raced by. She asked a big orange goldfish if he had seen the little fish who wanted wings. He just laughed and kept on swimming. Feeling discouraged, the dragonfly sat quietly on a lily pad to think and wonder about her little friend and his where-abouts.

The little fish sank deeper and deeper into the mud at the bottom of the pond. His breath grew slower and slower as his heart made fewer and fewer beats. Everything became very still and quiet, until one day he found himself watching a sunbeam glistening and darting in the water. It seemed to be filled with a voice, a beautiful voice—and then he knew! It was the lovely dragonfly calling through the sunlight!

"I must see her," he thought. So he lifted himself, feeling lighter than ever before, and moved in the sunlight to reach her. Just as he was about to break the water's surface, he saw her, more beautiful than he remembered. Seeing her wings, he felt his sadness, but not as before. He was sad about his wings, but very glad the beautiful dragonfly was free and had not been served for dinner to the Frog King.

At last, she saw him smiling at her beside the lily pad. She could see he had no wings, which caused her great feelings of sorrow. The dragon-fly asked the little fish why the Frog King had denied him his wish.

The little fish bowed his head in embarrassment and replied, "The king said I could have wings if I destroyed you and brought you to him for his meal. I couldn't do such a terrible thing, so I am as you see me today—without wings. It was a silly wish."

The dragonfly hid back her tears for she saw the true spirit of the little fish. "You did a very brave thing by giving up your dream for me. I will give you my wings. Come little fish, I will fly beneath you forever."

With that, the dragonfly gathered the little fish onto her back and they flew from the pond, over the meadows, above the treetops, and across the sky together.

After the little fish disappeared, it was said that all the little fishes born into the pond had wings.

Chapter 9

Still as Winter Woods

Sylvania and Sarah stood beside the water and stared at their reflections with the leaves gliding over them. It was very quiet until Sylvania spoke softly about the deep snow that covered the land. He told Sarah that if she could be as still as a winter woods, she would come to know herself. In silence, she would find her way.

Silence! The silence hurt Sarah's ears! She stuck her fingers in them to break the deafening sound and heard a soft drumming noise that thumped along in a steady rhythm. Sarah was listening to the beat of her own heart. "This is boring," she thought and removed her fingers. She turned to tell Sylvania, but he was gone! Her eyes searched out the woods but he was nowhere in sight. Looking for the path, she wondered why he had left her all alone.

The sun slid behind a cloud. She could feel it rather than see it. The cold penetrated her coveralls, making her dig into her pockets for her mittens. Jamming her hands into the wool protection, she stretched her legs into longer strides and picked up speed. The trees stood dark and foreboding against the white snow. Their branches loomed above her like wild hair against a steel-gray sky. Her breath blew in puffs, freezing against her cheeks. She could really feel her heart beat now! Fear propelled her from behind, giving her a strange feeling that she might outrun herself!

The thought of being caught in the woods with a storm approaching frightened her to the point of running her own race. She must get to Sylvania's house. Her feet made loud crunching sounds as they hit the icy spots and frozen ground. A hole, half hidden in the snow, caused Sarah to stumble and fall, bringing her close to tears. She quickly pulled herself upright, knowing she didn't have time to cry! It was growing darker by the minute. More snow was on the way!

Her toes were beginning to feel numb and the cold was getting colder. Sarah ran as fast as she knew how and called out, "Syl-va-nia," as often as she could while she kept her legs in motion.

Stopping to catch her breath, she leaned against a large oak tree, then curled herself within its roots to think about what she must do.

The solitude of the woods was growing as thick as her fear. She tried to remember what Sylvania was talking about before he left. It was something about being still and silence would help her find her way. So Sarah tried to do as he had told her. She listened to a woods awaiting snow and the stillness before it came. While taking in the quiet, she slipped her hands into her pockets for added warmth and noticed a small round object tucked into the corner of one of them. She pulled it out and saw to her surprise a tiny glass marble with a small "s" etched into its surface. It reminded Sarah of the glass ball Sylvania once lived in. She held it closer so she could see inside and there, before her eyes, was Sylvania looking at a map on a table. He was pointing to a direction. A star gleamed above the word North and a big black crow strutted across the paper. Sylvania tried to shoo it away, but it only flew off to return and sit on his shoulder.

Sarah couldn't believe it! There he was right before her eyes! Her dear old friend. He wasn't very far away from her after all! Now that she had her own magic ball, she could reach Sylvania when she needed him. But she had this very strange feeling that she was going to find her way on her own. Tucking the glass ball into her pocket, she stood up and thought about Sylvania reading a map and pointing to the direction of the north. She believed he was telling her to go that way but she wasn't sure where that was or how to get there. She looked all around, turned all around and finally looked up to the sky. There in the distance, beyond the clouds, a little star gleamed all alone. It was just like the one on Sylvania's map. Sarah knew she must go towards that small point of light.

Hurrying on through the woods, she kept her eyes lifted to the star, but forgot to look down at the ground. Suddenly, she tripped and fell. Taken by surprise, Sarah brushed the snow from her face to see what had caused her to lose her balance. A lovely straw basket sat a bit lopsided in the snow. She pulled it to her and looked inside where she found a large loaf of bread and a jug of milk. She quickly gobbled up the food and wondered who had left the basket for her when it suddenly occurred to her that it must have been the "secret people." Sylvania told her about them because she wanted to know who took care of him. He said they were little people who lived in the woods and performed good deeds without being seen. They moved about in magical, secretive ways. Sometimes, presents were left on the doorsteps as a surprise, or a need was met without it being asked for. Once, Sylvania went into the woods to gather firewood. When he returned to the house, a large load of wood was piled in the garden and the fireplace burned brightly. Sylvania was speechless! He knew the "secret people" had been there. In return, he always made sure extra food was left in the windowsills as well as a burning candle to welcome them. So Sarah was sure they were the ones who were secretly helping her.

Feeling refreshed, Sarah wiped her mitten across her mouth, stood up and looked for her star. It still shone in the distance as she took off for Sylvania's. Knowing the "secret people" were nearby, she felt safer in the woods. She felt as though she belonged there.

The walking had grown tiresome and she was beginning to feel sleepy. She knew better than to stop because it had grown colder than ever. She had to make herself move. Her arms and legs ached with weariness. Suddenly, out of nowhere, a black crow flew straight at her, then flew away to hide in the woods. That woke her up! "O.K. I'm awake!" she shouted. This seemed like an invitation because the crow made a surprise landing on her shoulder and continued to yell his "caw, caw" sounds in her ear. Sarah started to laugh. "I know you're trying to keep me awake. I promise, I'm wide awake!" So the black bird flew in front of her with its wide wings flapping while Sarah ran along behind.

Just when Sarah felt like giving up, they rounded a curve and came upon the little door in the hill. She stood before it in disbelief. She had made the long journey all by herself. "Well, almost by myself." she thought. Reaching for the handle, she pushed open the door and stepped into a garden filled with sunshine and golden day lilies swaying in the breeze. She could hear Sylvania banging on his pots and pans while he sang. "She's back. . .she's back. . .she has a knack. . .for finding her way back."

Sylvania marched into the garden and yelled, but it wasn't because he was glad to see Sarah. "Oh, no. I pushed the wrong button. I thought it said 'sing' but it was 'Spring'!"

Frantically, he dropped the pans and reached into his pocket for his instruction booklet on weather and seasons. Sarah began to scratch. Her mittens were beginning to itch. Pulling them off, she told Sylvania that she was glad he had made a mistake. "To me," she said, "it was like the garden knew of my coming and all the flowers and trees made ready. Thank you, Sylvania."

He put away his booklet and they turned, hand in hand to behold the spring-time view.

Chapter 10

Breaking the Spell

Sarah was walking under the hot sun. She could feel the heat on her back and the stream of perspiration roll salty into her mouth. Each step became slower and slower. She tried to make herself feel better by thinking about the coolness of the evening but that didn't work because she grew alone and afraid after the sun went down. At least it was daylight and she could see where she was going. So she returned to the path and trudged forward. Looking down, she noticed several bright white morning glories growing at her feet. She stared at their flowered whiteness. Suddenly, the road glowed like the morning sunrise sky. It was as if the blossoms were growing in the heavens.

"Sylvania, are you here? Are you hiding?" Sarah asked. "Are you playing a trick on me?"

As she swiftly turned around, a smiling Sylvania tiptoed from behind a tree and said, "It is a glorious morning, isn't it?"

Sarah grinned. "I knew it was you. Thought you had me fooled, didn't you?"

She kept on walking as Sylvania fell into step beside her. "I felt like. . . like I was seeing things," she said.

"You were, Sarah. And they were lovely things, too," he reminded her. "You saw the beauty of the morning in those glory-flowers. Did you know they close when the sunlight shines on them?"

Sarah shook her head back and forth. She didn't know about that.

"Well, you were lucky to see them open and full before they disappeared into themselves."

The two friends lowered their heads against the sun's glare as they moved down the road toward Sylvania's house. Sarah began to complain about the pressing heat and how she couldn't breathe in this kind of weather. It made her feel cross and crabby, too. Her mouth felt dry. She was wishing for a drink when Sylvania reached beneath his shirt and handed her a bottle of cold water. Surprised as always when he heard her unspoken wishes and granted her requests, she gulped down the refreshing liquid. Sarah licked her lips and expressed her gratitude in "whews" and "thank yous" as they continued their walk.

Sylvania pulled his mouth harp from his pocket and played a sweet song to lift their spirits and take their minds off the hot summer morning. Sarah tried to skip and dance a bit, but it didn't last long. Sylvania played a few more bars but stopped and stood still for a moment as if remembering something half forgotten.

"Sure would be nice to be cool, wouldn't it?" he said with a twinkle in his eye.

"That would be heaven!" she said.

"Well, that's where we're going." he laughed.

"To heaven!" she gasped.

"No, not that heaven. The one I'm thinking about is a neighbor's place and she calls it Heaven." I've been meaning to take you by there and this is just as good a time as any. Come on. Let's take a short cut through the honeysuckle. Be careful of the bees and snakes. Just follow me."

At the mention of snakes, Sarah let out a shriek and begged Sylvania to take her there another day. But Sylvania took her by the hand and gently led her along the path beyond the briars and honeysuckle vines. Sarah squinted, hoping it would prevent her from seeing any snakes. She kept telling herself that Sylvania knew the way and he would protect her, but she still felt uneasy.

The path spiraled upward and became rocky. When large boulders blocked their passage, they climbed over them, with Sylvania pulling her up onto the next level, twisting and turning, higher and higher. Sarah often asked, "Are we almost there?" To which Sylvania patiently replied, "Almost." A few moments later she would ask, "How much farther?" He would answer, "Not much."

The sunlight gave way to a cloudy day. Mists and haze made the climb slower. "I didn't know it was so hard to get to heaven." Sarah wheezed between steps. She heard Sylvania give a little chuckle as they slowly came to a ledge and looked down into a thick, grey carpet of fog.

Sylvania called out, "H-e-ll-o-o." All the l's and o's echoed in the woods behind them. As the last echo faded, the mists parted to reveal a tiny stone house suspended in the air beyond the cliff where they stood. A bridge of rope and boards swung to and fro. A sign hung at the entrance that read, "Heaven."

"Farther is no longer," said Sylvania. "I'll go first. Whatever you do, don't look down. Swing with the bridge. Move with the bridge. It's not as far away as it seems. Don't be frightened, now. Ready?"

"Ready?" Sarah thought–"Ready?" Fear kept her feet firmly rooted, frozen in place. What if she looked down? What would happen to her if she did? Were dragons lurking beneath the bridge to gobble her up with their green tongues?

She heard Sylvania's call to "hurr-e-e." He was disappearing into the fog as the bridge dipped low in the middle. Sarah knew she must follow. There was no turning back. She gritted her teeth and stepped onto the swinging bridge. When her feet touched the boards and her hands held the ropes, she was at once transported along a ribbony moonbeam that carried her with Sylvania to the front steps of the little house where they were deposited in a heap.

As they gathered themselves together, Sarah said in surprise, "Good night!" These seemed to be the magic words, because the door creaked open and they were ushered inside by a gust of wind.

Someone whispered, "Who goes there?" A dark figure stood before them. Sarah shivered. Sylvania greeted the person who stood in the silhouette and explained that he had brought along a friend to meet her. Sarah searched for the face within the folds of the blue-black mantle, but it remained hidden from her.

"Sarah, this is Moon Shadow Comes Walking," said Sylvania. Sarah stepped forward to meet the shadowed figure who moved back and explained, "I am the maiden of the mysterious. Welcome." She made a low bow which Sylvania and Sarah returned in kind. "Come, let us enjoy the evening." Sarah had never heard such an elegant voice. It was deep and rich, and smooth as silk.

The three of them proceeded to a window where Sylvania and Sarah stood behind the dark figure, gazing into a starlit night. The silky voice went on, "Why have you brought the child?"

"To break the spell," Sylvania replied.

"And what spell might that be?" inquired Moon Shadow Comes Walking. As the question was being spoken, Sarah knew the answer. She was afraid of the dark. When getting into bed, she feared someone was beneath it, ready to grab her by the ankle and pull her under, taking her away forever. She hesitated to open her closet door for fear someone would jump out and grab her. Most of all, she couldn't bear the light being turned out at bedtime, leaving her alone to face the monsters that lurked in the shadows of her room.

"Is this true?" asked the voice behind the veil.

"Yes. I am afraid of the dark," came Sarah's weak reply.

"Then you are afraid of me."

Sarah could feel the presence of Moon Shadow moving closer, speaking as she walked.

"We need the darkness so we may enjoy the day. The earth must have the dark to keep seeds quiet for rest and growth. The night gives us time to sleep and dream. The land must have shadow to provide the shade. If there were only day, we could never see the stars. All these things you know but the darkness makes you forget and you become afraid, don't you, Sarah?"

A tiny "yes" escaped Sarah's lips. Moon Shadow Comes Walking leaned down and placed a tiny crescent moon around Sarah's neck. "This is to help you to remember me and what I have said. It will ward off your fear of the dark. Wear it always." The moon glowed, making Sarah shine.

"Now, I want you to close your eyes. I will place my hand over them, giving you a new power. You will be able to see in the dark." Cool tender fingers caressed Sarah's eyes, filling them with bright green halos.

"You may look. Look at me," came the beautiful voice. Sarah's eyes fluttered open to gaze into emerald eyes and a face that shone softly through the darkness.

* * *

Sarah snuggled beneath the covers. It felt good to be in bed with the lights out, now that she could see in the dark. Feeling safe and warm she held the moon necklace in her hand and fell asleep.

Chapter 11

The Unfolding

Sylvania looked over the top edge of the book he was reading to Sarah and found her asleep before the dying fire. They had become good friends and their friendship had unfolded into one of trust and companionship which had changed them both. She was more willing to ask about the life around her as well as her own nature. He had become more challenged by her inquisitiveness. He was reminded of the time they took apart his clock to see how it worked because Sarah had never seen such an unusual timepiece. It was a water clock that had a drip for a tick. So they took it apart to look at its spits and spurts, much to the delight of them both. The memory made him smile as he watched her lying content in the branches of his wooden tree chair.

The book he had been reading slipped from his arms and slid to the floor. Through half-opened lids, he gazed at the orange and blue embers and thought about the times they had shared, the discoveries they had made, the cycles through which they had moved, and the seasons in which they had lived. It seemed to him it was all about a circle with no endings and no beginnings.

Sarah gave a little sigh as she nestled deeper into the chair. Sylvania brought a blanket from beside the fireplace and gently tucked its softness around the sleeping girl. As he returned to his seat and musings, he realized that he too had begun to marvel at the mysteries and unexplainable happenings that occurred more frequently when Sarah came for her visits. She had taught him to see with fresh eyes that looked in awe and wonder, even amazement. He smiled to himself, remembering the time they planted a tiny seed and watched for new green growth, but nothing had happened. All they saw was brown dirt for days and days. Finally, they gave up. Perhaps it was a "dud," one that was stunted without any possibility of becoming a plant. Then one day, Sarah was working in the garden and there it was. . .a stalk of green foliage that reached to the sky! She couldn't believe such a flower could come from one little seed. It was simply amazing to her that this had happened. She called it her Magic Flower.

With a deep breath, he took in the burning wood smell and exhaled a great A-a-a-ah sound which caused Sarah to stifle a yawn and mumble, "Where am I?"

"Safe and sound in your home away from home," replied Sylvania. Sarah rubbed her eyes to get the sleep out, but didn't quite succeed because she kept returning to a window where she saw her dream pulling her back.

She was playing ball, but the ball wasn't like any other ball she had ever seen before. A light seemed to live in the ball and it shone even brighter in the night. It was as big as a pumpkin and illuminated from within.

She ran after it. Just as soon as she reached down to hold it—the ball moved ahead, barely escaping her fingertips. Sometimes she played hide and seek with it. Quite often the ball rolled to her feet and then rolled right on by. The race continued.

Sometimes the ball appeared on rooftops or in open fields as if calling her to come and fetch it. She climbed over fences and forded small streams in search of the lit ball. Almost out of nowhere, the ball would appear.

She never grew tired of chasing the ball. It became a game. Surely she would have the ball and it would be hers, she kept telling herself. Until one day, the ball rolled towards her and she knew she could not play anymore. It was as if the ball heard her and stopped its rolling. They stood looking at one another. A voice came from the ball. "I am yours and you are mine."

The ball waited.

"I am yours and you are mine," she repeated. They came toward one another. She leaned down and took the ball into her arms.

It was then that she knew—it had been hers all along.

Chapter 12

The Gifts

She remembered her feelings of excitement because she had saved the best present for last. Sylvania had shared with her that he had broken his bow as a child and it had never been replaced. When he opened the gift and saw the magical white bow, he smiled like the boy he once had been. The surprise was worth the waiting. They laughed and danced in celebration. Then, in return, Sylvania placed a bouquet of roses in Sarah's arms to brighten a gray, mid-winter's day.

Gift giving was fun, especially when it came unexpectedly. Sarah ran to the cupboard to find a large container for the flowers while Sylvania practiced his aim with the new bow. When she returned, she felt alarmed as she watched him pull back the string and let it go. "You wouldn't shoot anything would you?"

Sylvania replied, "Only big bears when they come to the front door to eat little girls!" He thought this quite funny, while Sarah pretended not to see the humor. She was glad he wouldn't be shooting the wildlife and the bow and arrows would be used only for practicing with a target.

They walked down the steps and into the garden so Sylvania could practice shooting. He lifted the bow, placed an arrow in the string and released it into the forest beyond. They could hear the arrow zing as it flew through the air and out of sight. They paused in silence—waiting

45

for it to hit the ground—but there was not a sound. Sylvania shot a second arrow and the same thing happened. They stared at one another, not knowing what to think or do.

Suddenly a whirring sound came through the woods as one arrow stuck in the ground at their feet followed closely by the second. Sylvania lifted his bow and made another shot. That arrow landed beside the other two. Three arrows stood side by side.

Marching back and forth, Sylvania frowned and rubbed his whiskers and pondered this strange phenomenon. He thought and thought but was completely stumped. "Magical arrows that fly forward and backward?" All he could do was shake his head in dismay as he sat on the ground beside the arrows. Sarah took a seat beside him, every bit as puzzled as he.

The furrows in Sylvania's brow grew deeper and deeper. His frown hung heavy over his eyes while he searched for the meaning of the arrows that returned to the bowman—and suddenly he remembered a story he had once heard as a child. Of course! The answer was hidden there. He turned to Sarah and asked her if she would like to hear "The Tale of the Golden Arrows." He told her it might help them see behind the mystery of the arrows that flew without striking a target. Sarah clapped her hands, glad for a change of pace.

Sylvania began.

THE TALE OF THE GOLDEN ARROWS

Once upon a time there was a beautiful forest filled with animals and plants. It was lush and green with trees so tall they almost touched the sky. Everything prospered. The birds sang throughout the day while the deer came freely to drink by the stream. The beavers built high, strong dams to make waterfalls for the bears to play in while the fish hid in the dark pools. All the baby animals felt safe and happy in these woods.

One day the creatures heard a strange noise. It was a voice ringing sharply through the forest. It screeched and howled, frightening everyone and everything. The birds stopped singing, and the deer ran behind the trees, while the bears and beavers covered their ears to shut out the deafening shrill. As the voice grew nearer, the animals peered out to catch a glimpse of this wild and terrible thing. It was a little boy! He yelled at the trees and stomped on the ferns. He tore out the flowers beside the path and kicked rocks into the air, making dust clouds as he ran. On his back he carried a bow and a sheath of arrows which he used to stalk the creatures of the forest. This was his fun. He would shoot whatever he chose, leaving it wounded or dead.

He was an excellent marksman. He could shoot the legs off the birds as they sat perched on high branches and wound a rabbit while it bounded for cover, leaving it whimpering its last breath. He took delight in inflicting his power over the woodland animals. It made him feel big and strong.

One day while he ravaged the forest, the animals could stand it no longer. They had a Grand Council meeting and decided to build a trap for this boy who had no mercy on them. Everyone helped dig a giant hole. When they finished, the snails and spiders spun their trails and threads over it, making it look like a large puddle that glistened in the morning dew. They hid and waited.

Finally they heard him. The yowling and howling grew closer. The boy walked right into the trap. They could hear him scream as he fell to the bottom. The yelling ceased. All the animals gathered around the hole and stared into the dark pit where the boy lay still.

The animals turned away and made a quiet procession toward home. Several days later the boy awoke and found himself in the deep dark hole. He was thirsty and cold. His leg was twisted and broken. That night, in feverish perspiration, his dreams went wild. He heard the trees blowing rain down the sides of the dark pit. As he lay in the mud, three ghostly figures appeared before him. Each held an arrow. They spoke in unison.

"You have betrayed the spirit of the forest.

You have taken what is not yours.

You have caused suffering and pain."

The boy knew they had spoken the truth. He trembled before it. His head and leg told him about pain. The ghosts spoke to the boy of their sorrow in seeing what he had done with a bow and arrow. He shrieked and pleaded for pity on him, but they would not relent. They reminded him of how happy it had made him to bring about pain, to see the animals die and even to laugh at their distress. He could have helped, but he did not. The boy begged them to stop. They did not. They laughed as he had laughed.

When the boy could no longer endure the torment, he told them he was sorry. Only then did the ghosts become silent. "I am truly sorry," he whispered. "I will never do it again." The ghosts drew closer to see if he meant what he had said. They examined the boy and then conferred with each other. When they saw that the boy was sincere, they spoke once more in unison.

"Swear to protect the forest.

Give more to it than you take.

Heal rather than harm."

"I promise," he said.

The next morning, the sun shone into the hole where the boy lay. He opened his eyes to the glare. Three golden arrows lay on his chest in the sunlight; the promise returned to him.

The forest creatures stood around the rim of the hole. Everyone whispered. Even the birds chirped quietly. They had thought he was dead, but they could see he was not. Now they had to decide whether to help him or to let him die alone in the cold, dark hole. When the boy looked up, he saw them and yelled, "I've made a promise! I made a promise I will keep. I will never hurt you again. I will not ever shoot anything for the fun of it. I will be a friend to you. Please help me. Oh, please help me."

Everyone murmured their doubt except their leader, a large buck who believed the boy had learned his lesson. He said, "We must give the boy a chance. Let's all hold on to one another and I'll lean into the hole and pull him out with my antlers." He was so persuasive that everyone agreed. So it was that they rescued the boy from the hole, cared for his wounds, and made him whole once again.

From that day forward, the forest returned to a bountiful and beautiful place where the boy could be seen shooting his golden arrows at the empty sky or across the hills. By aiming at nothing, he brought the arrows back to him, where they fell at his feet.

Chapter 13

Door of Tomorrow

Sylvania laid the ring of keys on the table while he spoke to Sarah about looking at the simple made beautiful in everyday life. Sarah was hearing the words, but she was only half listening; she couldn't keep her eyes off the keys. They glistened and twinkled as if calling her to their attention. She suddenly remembered the locked door in the hallway. All the other rooms were open to her, but this one was locked. She was lost in wondering about what lay beyond the locked door and if one of the golden keys could unlock it. As she thought about the dilemma, Sylvania continued to speak more about the ways to look and see.

She tried to listen, but the locked door occupied her thoughts. "Sarah. . .Sarah?" Sylvania called out to her.

"Yes?" she replied dreamily.

"Come down to earth! he called. "You seem to be far away."

Sarah tried to sit up straighter and look more attentive, but she could not stop thinking about the locked door and the golden keys. Sylvania cleared his throat and gave an obvious little cough, hoping to call her back. He began to grumble about her losing interest. Finally, she asked the question that was on her mind all along. "Why is the door down the hall locked?"

Sylvania's eyes flew wide open. He huffed and puffed. The silence grew in volumes, making Sarah uncomfortable. She began to twitch and rub her shoes together while Sylvania stared without making a comment. She wished she hadn't asked. She thought it was a simple question with a simple answer. But now she knew better.

Following a few attempts to explain, Sylvania replied quite simply, "Because it is the Door of Tomorrow. Through that door the future makes itself known."

Now it was Sarah's turn to be surprised. "Uh. . .You mean, if it's unlocked and you walk inside, you get to know your future?"

"You bet," he said.

Sarah jumped from her chair and ran down the hall toward the locked door with Sylvania calling, "Not so fast. You haven't got the key!"

She dashed back to him and pulled his arms and pleaded with him to take her through the Door of Tomorrow. But Sylvania only shook his head at her impatience, while remaining in his seat.

"Oh, please, come on. It'll be okay. I want to find out all about what I'll be when I grow up. I want to see into the future! What fun!"

Sylvania just looked at her and continued to sit. Frustrated and pouting, Sarah returned to her chair and flopped herself into it with a scowl.

Sylvania tried to point out that looking into tomorrow was a very serious undertaking which took a great deal of preparation and readiness. He asked Sarah if she really thought she was ready to see what the future held. This made her think. What if she discovered some scary things and she became frightened not only of tomorrow but the next day and the next. What if she discovered some things that were wonderful, grand and exciting? Maybe she would marry a prince and become a queen. Then again, what if she discovered she was marrying a wart hog and every time he touched her, she broke out in big ugly bumps. Maybe it wasn't such a good idea—at least not right now, anyway. Sylvania's voice pulled her back into the moment.

"It's important to be in the world, Sarah. The rest will take care of itself. The real key is in the knowing of today." he said. She realized she didn't see the point, until Sylvania began to talk about his garden and a lovely flower that grew there. He guided her mind around its petaled edges, spoke of the crimson center that bled into its pure whiteness and how the stamen rose gold and yellow. He told her how bees loved to buzz within its sweetness and of the aroma the flower gladly shared.

Sarah sat quietly listening to Sylvania roll along about every day things made special when she had a thought. . . Sylvania was helping her to imagine the flower, so. . . Maybe the future is about imagining your life and you in it! She remembered when she first met Sylvania and the sign that read IMAGINE. "Maybe I can imagine my life and make it come true for myself!" she thought. Suddenly bells rang, making her look around the room to see who had rung them. But she didn't see any bell ringers. Could it be that her thoughts had been heard?? She looked at Sylvania and noticed his suspenders had tiny silver bells attached to them. He smiled at her in his knowing way.

Then she remembered the DOOR OF TOMORROW—and was struck with another thought, maybe—just maybe the future was a tomorrow becoming today. Again. . .bells rang. In fact the whole room was filled with the sound of ringing bells. It was then, she knew that was how the door would open to her—tomorrow would become today and the future would become now. She would be there to see it come and go. Sarah hopped down from her chair, gave Sylvania a hug and left for the garden to watch the goldfish play and swim in the waters of the blue fountain.

Chapter 14

Firelight

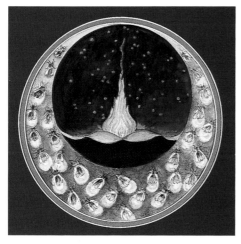

It felt warm and comfortable sitting with Sylvania before the hearth, watching the sparks fly up the chimney. Her eyes slowly drifted into the flames and wood. She felt sleepy, remembering other sleepy times when she looked out the bedroom window into the meadow where the fireflies danced in the darkness.

She watched the fire closely, studying the logs for pictures. It was a game she had played for a long time, much like the one where she lay on the ground and watched the clouds for shapes of faces and animals. POW! The fire popped as a log rearranged itself, causing Sarah and Sylvania to jump and then laugh at themselves for being startled. Turning back to the fire, Sylvania puffed on his pipe and Sarah gathered her blanket closer, tucking the corners around her toes. Fire watching seemed to be a favorite pastime for both of them.

Tonight, the flames burned low and hovered among the embers, bringing the little flame people into view. Sarah watched as they danced in their brightly colored costumes of blue, purple, and orange. There seemed to be some invisible music that brought them alive and taught them the rhythms of a song that lay hidden within the hearth. Their voices could be heard as they sang its phrases among the logs that hissed and howled in accompaniment. The smoke twirled in gray spiraling circles, pulling the dancers along the wood and deeper into the dance. Occasionally, the wind blew down the chimney in great billowing rushes, momentarily smothering the dance and causing the dancers to disappear. The fire smoldered, deep and quiet, creating an interlude within the dance. Often alone, without a partner, one of the little flame dancers would appear. It seemed to gather others as it carried the dance that began again. They flickered in unison to the silent pulse, dancing together, then gathering; then standing tall and glorious as one bright torching light. But, the stance of the single light was brief, only to be replaced by another and yet another. They burned brightly for the finale; then burned not at all. A back light of deep orange-red moved along the fireplace floor without a sound, intensifying the solitude of the room's darkness.

The dance took on an eerie quality as the dancers danced themselves into the coals and vanished, while the silent beat went on. The flame people left for their home beyond the sky, leaving a tired old man and a dreamy young girl asleep before the ebbing warmth.

Chapter 15

Farewell to the Sylvan

A hint of Fall was in the air and a tinge of yellow clung to the trees. She ran hard and fast to get to the bridge over the river that ran past Sylvania's house. She wanted to go there to think about the trip she and her grandmother were taking away from the woods. The thought of it brought a sick queasy feeling to the bottom of her stomach.

Once there, she stopped to catch her breath and admire the beauty of the tall tree beside the bridge. Standing in its shade, she thought about how much she would miss Sylvania while she was away, but she reminded herself of her newly acquired magic ball, so perhaps, the time away from him would not be so hard. They could talk with one another through their glass globes to ease the loneliness.

Hoisting herself over the edge of the bridge wall, she looked down into the waters below, remembering their days together. The memories floated by with the river, making her feel sad at their passing. But old memories are replaced with new ones, so she thought about all the times to come; the new adventures to be shared and the stories to be told. She knew he would be waiting for her in the little house hidden in the hill.